First published in Great Britain in 2001.
This edition published in 2006 by Brimax Publishing Ltd
Appledram Barns, Birdham Road, Chichester, PO20 7EQ, UK
© Brimax Publishing Ltd

Printed in China

Can't, Shan't, Won't!

BRIMAX

In a land of ice and snow,
where the wild wind blows, live three very
naughty penguins. They are called
Can't, Shan't, and Won't.
Whenever Mother Penguin asks the little
rascals to help her, they shuffle
and slither away as fast as they
can on their slippery,
flippery feet, and
pretend not to hear her.

Today Mother Penguin wants the little
penguins to catch some fish for supper.
As soon as they hear her calling,
"Can't . . . Shan't . . . Won't!"
the naughty penguins race down the slippery
slide and hide in an ice cave.
But Mother Penguin is pretty good at sliding
too, and very good at finding ice caves,
so she soon tracks them down.

"Now!" gasps Mother Penguin,
shaking the snow from her flipper-like
wings and panting for breath.
"I need your help. You must catch
some big, fat, juicy fish for supper."
The three little penguins
look up at her sadly.

"Can't," says Can't.
"My flippers are too cold."
"Shan't!" says Shan't. "My feet are too cold."
"Won't!" says Won't. "My beak is too cold."
"Nonsense!" says Mother Penguin.
"You are penguins. You like the cold!
Now, here are your fishing
rods – on your way!"

So the three little penguins slide
off across the snow. Icy Lake is always
frozen over, but every now and then there
are little round holes that the seals use
to come up for air. These holes are perfect
places for patient penguins to catch fish.
But Can't, Shan't, and Won't are not
patient. They cannot sit still
for a minute.

"I can't *see* why we should sit here,"
says Can't, after just one minute,
peering into the hole.
"I shan't *be able* to catch a thing with this
tangled line," says Shan't, after just two
minutes.
"I won't ever *be* warm again," says Won't,
after just three minutes,
shivering from his *beak* to his feet.
"Let's go home!"
shout Can't, Shan't, and Won't.
So they set off across the ice,
without a single fish.

"Can't go home without fish, Mother will
be angry," says Can't, slipping on the ice.
"Shan't have anything for supper!"
says Shan't, sliding down an icy bank.
"Won't go home again,"
says Won't, skating on one foot.
So they decide to run away!

The little penguins skip and scamper all the way to where the icy land meets the sea. There they jump onto an iceberg, and before very long, the iceberg slides away, floating along on the waves.

The little penguins are very scared.
"What's your name?" asks an old walrus.
"Can't!" cries Can't. "Can't ever stop!"
"What's your name?" asks a snowy seal.
"Shan't!" sobs Shan't.
"Shan't ever get home!"
"What's your name?" booms a huge whale.
"Won't!" weeps Won't.
"Won't ever run away again!"

Still the iceberg sails on. Soon it
is dark, and the moon rises over the
snow-capped sea. It is very cold, and
by now the penguins are very, very scared!
Then suddenly the wild wind begins to blow.
It blows the iceberg in a circle.
It blows the iceberg across the waves.
It blows the iceberg back to shore,
where the icy land meets the sea.
And there, waiting for the
little penguins, is Mother.

"Thank goodness you're safe!"
She hugs each little penguin in turn.
"We were lost!" cries Can't.
"We were cold!" sobs Shan't.
"And we don't have any fish!" weeps Won't.
"Never mind," says Mother Penguin.
"Father has caught plenty, so we can have
a nice fish supper. Let's go home."
Off they ride on Father's sled, back to
their warm, safe house in the snow.

After supper, Mother tucks the penguins
into their warm, cozy bed.
"I can't believe we were so silly," sighs Can't.
"I can," laughs Mother Penguin.
"We shan't run away again,"
mumbles Shan't.
"Home is the best place to be,"
agrees Mother.
"And we won't ever be naughty again!"
yawns Won't, with just a hint of a twinkle
in his one open eye.
"We'll see!" smiles Mother Penguin.
"Sweet dreams, Can't, Shan't, Won't".